Funny Names

By

Toni McPants

KANYIE MEDIA

Published by KANYIE MEDIA
PO Box 75031, London, SW14 9DE

Originally published in Great Britain in 2019
by Kanyie Media.

www.OddNameTown.com
www.KanyieMedia.com

Odd Name Town Books

CONTENTS

Welcome to Odd Name Town, where strange is normal and normal is strange. Everyone has a funny name.

Jack Pot is very lucky. When strange things start happening in Odd Name Town, Jack solves the mysteries with his two best friends, Kerry Oki and Joe King.

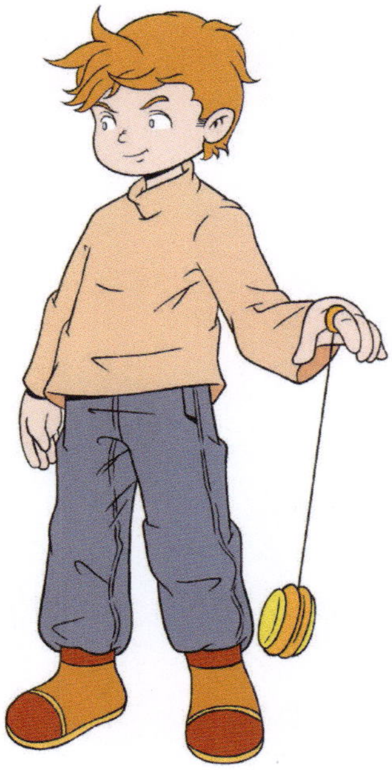

Kerry Oki loves singing karaoke. She likes playing the cello, doing ballet and karate, but she has to carry *all* her bags to school every day.

That's not always easy when TROUBLE is lurking.

Joe King loves joking. When Joe is not telling one of his famous jokes, he is thinking of one.

Bobby Bruiser is the biggest bully in town. He terrorizes everyone with his two friends Little Ike and Brutal Brutus. That's not all, Bobby has an evil dog called Bonzo.

Little Ike and Brutal Brutus are Bobby's menacing best friends.

Little Ike is not so little.

Brutal Brutus is extra brutal.

Bonzo is Bobby Bruiser's vicious big dog.

Bonzo is the bone-crunching, bottom-biting, leg munching, underpants eating, mean dog that frightens everyone.

Tom Katt and **Aly Katt** are the naughty twins. They like eating cookies, but love stealing even more.

The twins always get caught, because they leave A LOT of cookie crumbs behind and they fight a lot.

Rob Banks is always robbing banks. Sometimes he steals with his two best friends, Aly and Tom Katt.

Tom Katt, **Aly Katt** and **Rob Banks** are not good thieves, because they always get caught and end up in Cell 57 at Odd Name Town Prison.

Officer B. Ware is the Police Chief. When there is trouble in town, she is there to stop it.

Beware of Officer B. Ware!

Mayor M.T. Head is the Mayor of Odd Name Town. Everyone thinks Mayor M.T. Head has an empty head, because he is *always* forgetting.

Miss Moo Dee is the moody Milk Lady. She is usually happy when she is delivering milk, but gets very moody when Bonzo chases her.

Mr D Liver, the Postman, delivers letters in town. He is Bonzo's favorite target.

All of Mr D. Liver's pants have holes.

Mrs Chalkstick is the best teacher in Odd Name Town School.

Mrs Dinah Soare is the world's oldest librarian. She is so old, no one knows how old she really is. Some say Mrs Dinah Soare is older than the dinosaurs.

Farmer Don Key loves animals. He has many different animals at his farm, but Farmer Don Key's favorite is, his donkey.

Mr Sonny Day and **Mrs Holly Day** are always going on sunny holidays. Sonny and Holly have been to all the countries in the world.

Jim Sox is the school gym teacher. Jim Socks is always wearing his gym socks and shouting in the gym.

Candy Barr is the sweet seller. His shop is filled with many yummy sweets.

Doctor Hurt is the friendly town doctor, but everyone is scared to visit the doctor.

Mark A Roni works in the Italian restaurant. Chef Mark A. Roni makes the most delicious macaroni dish in town.

Pepe Roni makes the best pizza maker in town. His favorite topping is extra peperoni.

Mr Bill Ding builds all the buildings in Odd Name Town.

Brock Lee is the Green Grocer. Brock sells different fruit and vegetables, but everyone loves his broccoli.

Mrs Daisy Pot is Jack's mother. She works at the Flower Shop.

Otto Graf is a famous movie star. When Otto Graf is not acting or having his pictures taken, he is signing autographs for his fans.

Tim Burr is a woodworker and carpenter. When he cuts down a tree, he shouts, "TIMBER"!

Sue Yoo is Odd Name Town's best lawyer. If you upset her, she might sue you.

Justin Time is the coolest bus driver. Justin Time is never late, he is always just in time.

Rusty Keys can fix anything and everything. Rusty always has his big old wrench with him.

Miss Dazzle is the Arts Teacher. She loves to make shiny things.

Mrs Bacon is the school cook.

They say, "The early bird catches the worm," but, **Earl E. Bird** is always early for everything, sometimes way too early.

Mona Lott and **Noah Lott** are the stuck-up rich twins. Everyone calls them the Rah-Rah twins, because they like to say, "Rah Rah" after every sentence.

Mona Lott likes to moan a lot and **Noah Lott** thinks he knows a lot.

Myles Long is the tallest boy in school.

Hazel Nutt likes eating nuts, especially hazelnuts.

Collie Flower is always happy. Her hair is always tied up into buns.

Anna Conder has a pet anaconda snake. Anna takes her pet snake everywhere, including school.

Paige Turner loves reading books. Paige is always turning pages.

Marsha Mellow likes eating marshmallows.

Poppy Seeds will eat anything with poppy seeds in it.

Rick Shaw is the fastest bike rider. He is always whizzing and speeding through Odd Name Town.

Anita Cuddle loves hugging and cuddling. Anita Cuddle always needs a cuddle.

Pete Sake is super clumsy. He breaks everything and falls over nothing. "Oh, for Pete's sake!"

Printed in Great Britain
by Amazon

14887520R00022